monkey mayhem!

Written by Ronne Randall
Illustrated by Jacqueline East

Bright Sparks ☆

Mickey and Maxine Monkey had finished their breakfast of Mango Munch. Now they were rushing off to play.

"Be careful!" called their mom. "And DON'T make too much noise!"

"We won't!" the two mischevious monkeys promised, leaping across to the next tree.

"WHEEE," screeched Mickey.

"WA-HOOOO!" hollered Maxine.

The noise echoed through the whole jungle—
Mickey and Maxine just didn't know how to be quiet!

KA-THUNK! Mickey landed on a branch.

KA-CLUNK!

Maxine landed beside him.

KER-AACK!

"OOOHHH NOOOO!"

the monkeys hollered as the branch snapped in two.

"YI-I-IKES!"

they shrieked, as they went tumbling down, down, down.

KER-THUMMPPP!
SPROI-OI-OING!

The jungle shook as the two monkeys crashed to the ground, then sprang to their feet.

"YIPPPEEEEEE!" the monkeys cheered, brushing themselves off.

"That was so much FUN!" exclaimed Maxine. "Let's go get Chico Chimp and see if he wants to do it, too!"

Chattering as they went, the two monkeys scrambled back up to the tree tops.

"HEY, CHICO! COME AND PLAY WITH US!" they bellowed as they swung through the branches toward the chimps' house.

All through the jungle, animals shook their heads and covered their ears. Couldn't anyone keep those naughty, noisy monkeys quiet?

Chico Chimp was soon ready to play with his friends. The three of them had a great time swinging, tumbling, and bouncing together. Then they spotted a coconut palm.

"Hey!" shouted Chico. "Let's get some coconuts!"

"Great!" said Maxine. "Last one up the tree is a rotten banana!"

But before they got to the coconut palm, they stopped short. Grandpa Gorilla was standing in their path, glaring at them angrily.

"Get going, you mischief-makers," he said. "You've given everyone enough headaches for one day. My grandson Gulliver is fast asleep down by the river, and if you wake him up, I will be very, very upset!"

"Sorry," whispered Maxine, looking down at the ground. Everyone in the jungle knew it was a big mistake to upset Grandpa Gorilla!

"We'll be quiet," the three friends promised.

Mickey, Maxine and Chico didn't know what to do. Then Mickey said, "Let's just climb the tree. We can do that quietly.

"Okay," the others agreed half-heartedly.

"I suppose it's better than doing nothing," said Maxine.

From their perch up among the coconuts, the three friends could see what was happening all over the jungle.

They saw Jerome Giraffe showing his son Jeremy how to choose the juiciest, most tender leaves on a tree...

...and they saw Portia Parrot giving her daughter Penelope her first flying lesson.

And right below them, they saw little Gulliver Gorilla sleeping contentedly in the tall grass beside the river.

And – uh-oh! They saw something else, too. Claudia Crocodile was in the river. She was grinning and snapping her big, sharp teeth – and heading straight for Gulliver!

The three friends didn't think twice. Maxine shouted,

"GET UP, GULLIVER! GET UP RIGHT NOOOOWW!"

At the same time, Mickey and Chico began throwing coconuts at Claudia.

SMAACCCKK!

THWAACKK! went the coconuts.

they went, right on Claudia's hard crocodile head.

"OWW-WOOWW" moaned Claudia.

"OWW-WOW OWW-WOW!"

"What's going on here?" Grandpa Gorilla shouted up into the coconut tree. "I thought I told you three to keep quiet!"

All the noise woke Gulliver. The little gorilla sat up, looked around, and ran to his grandpa, who was hurrying toward the river.

Then he saw Claudia swimming away, and he realized what had happened. He grabbed Gulliver and gave him a great big gorilla hug. "I'm so glad you're safe!" he said.

Maxine, Mickey, and Chico came down from the tree.

"We're sorry we made so much noise," Chico said.

By this time all the other gorillas had gathered round, and so had most of the other jungle animals.

"What's all the commotion about?" asked Jerome Giraffe.

"Yes, what's going on?" squawked Portia Parrot.

"These three youngsters are heroes," said Grandpa.
"They saved my grandson from being
eaten by Claudia Crocodile!"

"Hurrah!" cheered all the other animals.
Mrs. Monkey and Mrs. Chimp beamed with pride.

"I think you deserve a reward," said Grandpa Gorilla. "And I think your reward should be..."

All the other animals held their breath in anticipation.

PEEEEE!"

cheered Mickey, Maxine, and Chico, in their loudest, screechiest voices. Their grins were almost as wide as the river.

"OH, NOOOOOO!"

all the other animals groaned together – but they were all smiling, too.